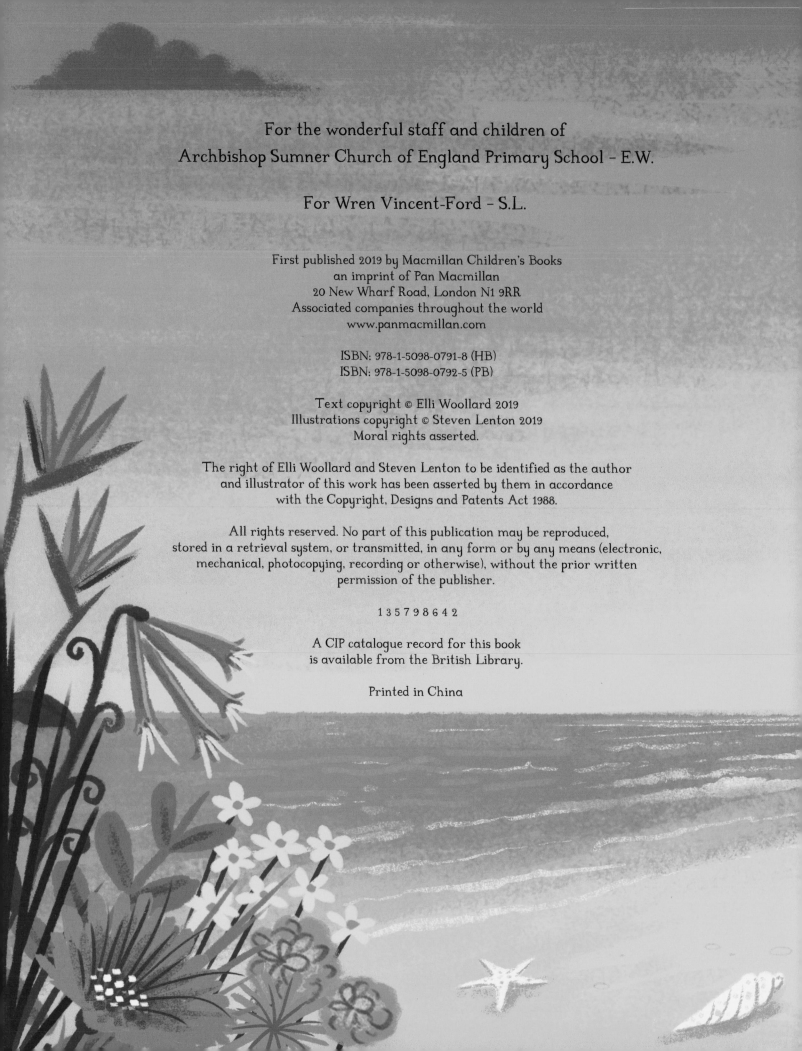

For the wonderful staff and children of
Archbishop Sumner Church of England Primary School – E.W.

For Wren Vincent-Ford – S.L.

First published 2019 by Macmillan Children's Books
an imprint of Pan Macmillan
20 New Wharf Road, London N1 9RR
Associated companies throughout the world
www.panmacmillan.com

ISBN: 978-1-5098-0791-8 (HB)
ISBN: 978-1-5098-0792-5 (PB)

1 3 5 7 9 8 6 4 2

A CIP catalogue record for this book
is available from the British Library.

Printed in China

DILLY the DONKEY

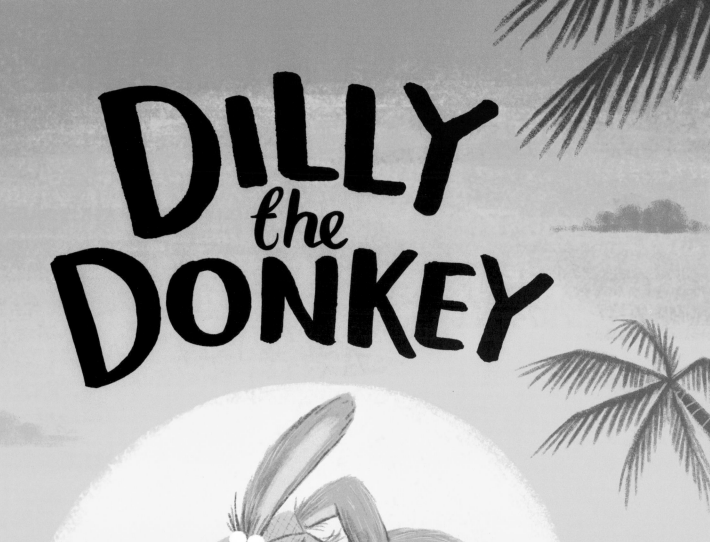

Written by
Elli Woollard

Illustrated by
Steven Lenton

MACMILLAN CHILDREN'S BOOKS

On a track by the sand in a spice-scented land,
Where the breezes blew beautifully cool,
Dilly the donkey, little and wonky,
Carted the children to school.

She limped, she was bent,
but she sang as she went,

"Hee haw,
hee haw"

through the town.

She loved it a lot (trit trot, trit trot),
Till her owner came up, with a frown:

"You're plodding and slow and quite old, don't you know,
And besides, you sound noisy and coarse.
And since that's the case, I will buy, in your place,
A most wonderful winsome young . . .

The horse started dancing, and preening, and prancing,

She hurried and scurried and skipped,

While the donkey went fumbling and stumbling and tumbling,
She hobbled and wobbled and tripped.

"You're quite a disaster! Move faster! Move faster!"
The owner said, shaking his head.

So the horse pulled the cart, looking stylish and smart,
While poor Dilly was shoved in a shed.

"It's really not fair!" she wailed in despair.
"Be useful? I'm sure that I could.
Yet I'm wonky and grey, I've a horrible bray,
So maybe I'm simply no good."

But later that night, with the moon beaming bright,
Came two robbers who muttered, "oho!"

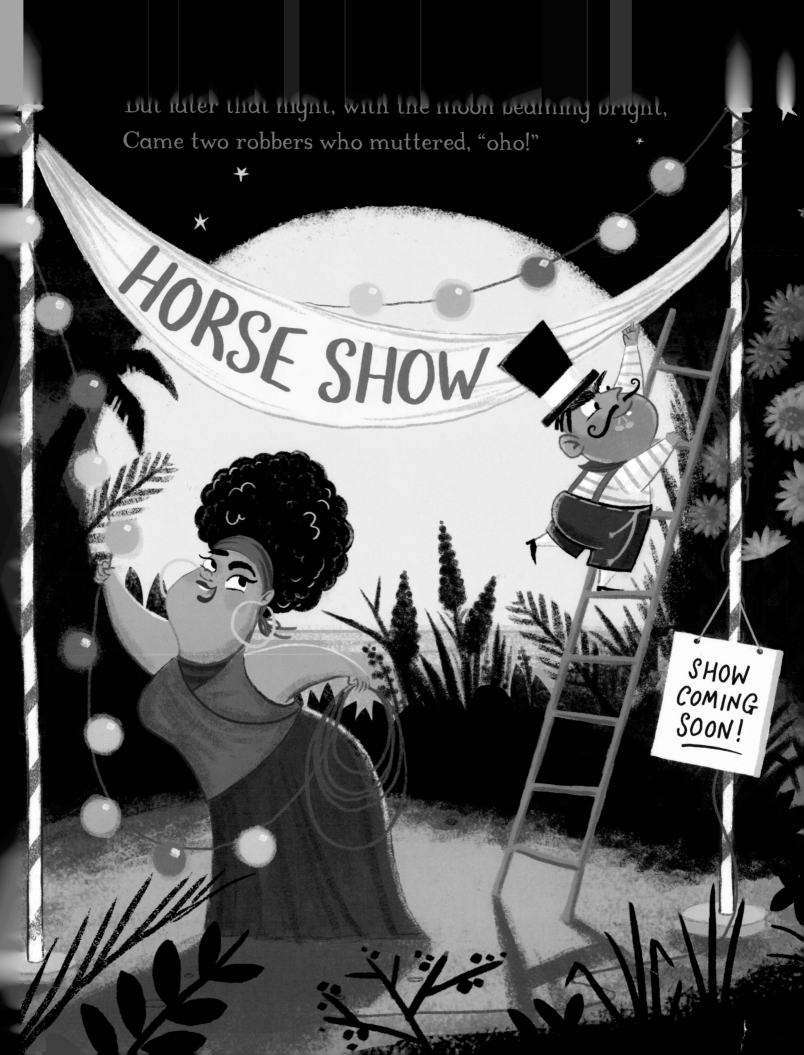

"When the coast is all clear, let's come robbing, my dear!
We will steal that new horse for our show!

She will daintily dance, she will prettily prance,

And scamper   and skitter and skip.

We'll work her all day
and she'll do as we say.

If not, we will show her the whip!"

As the thieves slipped away, Dilly stirred in the hay,
And she stared at the stars in great awe.
"I'm wonky and small, but perhaps, after all
I can help. Hee haw! Hee haw!"

And so in the morning she gave out a warning,
A terrible ear-splitting bray.
But the owner just laughed, "Oh Dilly, you're daft!

'Hee haw!' Is that all you can say?"

The next day at ten, she tried once again,
She wrote a short note in the sand.

Robbers - there's proof! she wrote with a hoof,
But her owner did not understand.

So desperate, alone, she found an old phone,
And she dialled '999' for a cop.

Yet nobody came when she brayed out her name,

And she fell to the floor with a flop.

"I tried, I tried, I tried," Dilly cried.
"But now it's too late – there's no hope!"
And the robbers came back when the skies turned to black
And they cut, with a 'snap!' the mare's rope.

"Oho!" they yelled. "Let's go!" they yelled,
As they chortled and chuckled with glee.
"With this horse in our show how our money will flow!
Oh, how beautifully rich we'll soon be!"

The horse, of course, went clippety clop,
As the robbers rode off down the street.

While Dilly the donkey, little and wonky,
Followed on faltering feet.

"A-ha!" they cheered, "a-ha!" they jeered,
"We've brilliantly beaten the law."

But then round a bend,
their hair stood on end –

"Nee naw,
nee naw,
nee naw!"

"Police!" they shrieked, "police!" they squeaked,

And into the darkness they ran.

"Yes!" shouted Dilly, "I'm not simply silly!
Be useful? Of course - yes I CAN!"

Her owner said, "Wow! Did *you* do that? How?
Oh Dilly, you're ever so clever!
But still little donkey, you're slow and you're wonky,
I simply can't keep you forever.

You're smart and you're brave," he said, as he gave her
A medal that glimmered like gold.

"But now, Dilly dear, I *must* make this clear,
You're not staying here . . .

. . . you've been
SOLD."

On a track by the sand in a spice-scented land,
Where the waves wash the shimmering shore,
Dilly the donkey, little and wonky,
Doesn't pull carts any more.

FOUND!

She slips and she slows, but she sings as she goes,
Her bray ringing out through the peace.
And she loves it a lot (trit trot, trit trot) . . .

Now she works for the chief of police.